Recording the Past

written by Michael Burgan

illustrated by Dick Smolinski

McGraw-Hill
School Division

New York   Farmington

Billy raced through the living room, his sister, Jean, tearing after him.

"Hand over that tape recorder!" Jean yelled. "I want to play some music."

"Forget it," Bobby said, ducking behind the couch. "I'm going to tape myself making weird noises."

"Every time you open your mouth you make weird noises," Jean said, leaping at Billy and tackling him.

"What's all this noise in here?" a voice cried.

Jean and Billy stopped and looked up. Their grandmother gazed down at them, her hands on her hips.

"Oh, hi, Babci," Billy said with growing embarrassment."We were just, uh, playing."

"Playing?" Babci repeated. "I don't think so.
You two were fighting again, weren't you?"

Jean asked, "Oh, Babci, didn't you fight
with your brothers and sisters?"

"Yeah," Billy said, "like over what TV show
to watch or who got to use the computer."

Their grandmother laughed. "Computers and
TVs? When I was a girl in Poland, we didn't
have those things. In fact, we didn't even have
electricity."

"No electricity!" Billy and Jean said at the same time.

"No, life was different back then. I can't imagine I've never told you what my life was like back in Poland. But anyway, how would you like to hear about it now?"

"Wait a minute, Babci," said Billy. "I'll be right back."

Billy came back with a cassette and handed it to his grandmother along with the tape recorder. "Here, Babci," he said, "let's tape your story."

Babci examined the machine suspiciously. "You'd better do it," she said, setting it down on the coffee table.

Billy popped in the tape, pushed the buttons, and looked at Babci.

Babci began. "When I was a young girl, all I knew about was working on a farm." Babci stopped and pointed at the recorder. "It's on?" she asked.

"Yes," Billy said, as he and Jean settled in at Babci's feet.

"We lived outside a town called Bransk. It was such a lovely town with quaint wooden houses and wonderful shops. There was a beautiful river that ran through it. It was such a treat to go with Papa to Bransk when he brought eggs and produce to the market.

"You see, on our farm we raised some chickens and grew potatoes and beets."

"Beets!" Billy said. "Yuck! I hate beets."

"I'm not so crazy about beets either," Babci said, "but when you're hungry, you eat beets."

"Did you have to work in the fields with your parents?" Jean asked.

"Yes," Babci replied. "So did my three brothers and four sisters. My father rented the land from a wealthy man who lived in town. We ate some of the crops we harvested and sold the rest."

"When did you live in Poland?" Billy asked. "A hundred years ago?"

"Oh, Billy. I'm not that old!" cried Babci. "We left Poland in 1939, when I was nine years old. You can figure out the math, can't you?"

Billy nodded and did some counting on his
fingers. Then he asked, "What chores did you
have to do on the farm, Babci?"

"Mostly I picked potatoes, which is really
dirty work. My brother Stosh dug up the
ground, while I was on my hands and knees,
pulling potatoes out of the soil."

"Ugh," Jean said. "That sounds so gross. But
you didn't work all the time, did you, Babci?
You must have had some fun, even if you didn't
have electricity."

"Of course we had fun," Babci said with a smile. "After dinner my father told stories and we sang songs.

"The most fun we had was when we went to the annual festival in Bransk. We stuffed ourselves with pierogis and freshly cured ham and danced polka after polka. All the girls wore their best clothes. Of course, we had to make our own."

"You made your own clothes?" Jean said.

"Well, sure," said Billy. "They didn't have any malls, right, Babci?"

"No malls," Babci said. "My mother was lucky enough to have an old sewing machine. To make it work, you had to press pedals. One year I wanted a new traditional folk costume for the festival. She helped me make a beautiful skirt and blouse, which we decorated with a pattern of red and gold.

"Then, when the big day came, my mother went up into our tiny attic. She came back with a beautiful silver pin that had belonged to her mother. It was the only piece of jewelry my mother owned, and she gave it to me to wear to the festival. I was so proud."

Billy looked at Babci's dress. "That silver pin you're wearing now?" he asked.

Babci nodded. "Someday soon I will give it to your mother, and one day, Jean, your mother will give it to you. When you wear it, you'll think of her, of me, of my mother, and of her mother before her."

"Babci, thank you!" Jean jumped up and hugged her grandmother.

"Okay," Billy said. "No more mushy stuff. Finish your story, Babci."

"There's not much left to tell. My father was anxious to leave Poland. He hadn't gone to school, but he was a smart man.

"Papa heard that Germany, which is right next to Poland, was getting ready to go to war. He thought Germany's army would invade Poland. We packed up whatever we could carry and left our farm to come to America.

"So here I am. And here you are, too."

Babci looked at the tape recorder. "Is that thing still going?"

"Yeah," said Billy. "And I bet it got every word."

"Good. You make sure you keep that tape," said Babci.

"I will," Billy said. "Jean can have your pin, but I'll always have your memories."